Contents

KU-407-910

FK ROB
NEWCASTLE-UNDER-LYME
COLLEGE LEARNING
RESOURCES
DC028707

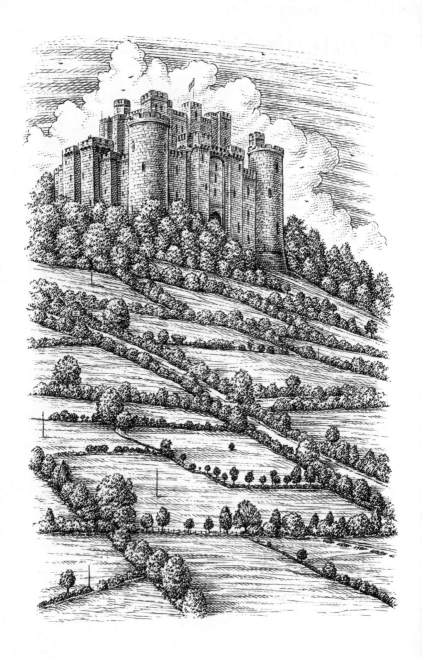

ase return this book on or before the last date
stamped below.

Down in the Dungeon

Brandon Robshaw

NEWCASTLE-UNDER-LYME
COLLEGE LEARNING
RESOURCES

Published in association with
The Basic Skills Agency

Hodder & Stoughton

A MEMBER OF THE HODDER HEADLINE GROUP

Newcastle Under Lyme College

DC028707

Acknowledgements
Cover: George Smith
Illustrations: Dave Hopkins

Orders: please contact Bookpoint Ltd, 130 Milton Park, Abingdon, Oxon OX14
4SB. Telephone: (44) 01235 827720, Fax: (44) 01235 400454. Lines are open from
9.00 - 6.00, Monday to Saturday, with a 24 hour message answering service.
Email address: orders@bookpoint.co.uk

British Library Cataloguing in Publication Data
A catalogue record for this book is available from The British Library

ISBN 0 340 84844 8

First published 2002
Impression number   10 9 8 7 6 5 4 3 2 1
Year   2005 2004 2003 2002

Copyright © 2002 Brandon Robshaw

All rights reserved. No part of this publication may be reproduced or
transmitted in any form or by any means, electronic or mechanical, including
photocopying, recording, or any information storage and retrieval system,
without permission in writing from the publisher or under licence from the
Copyright Licensing Agency Limited. Further details of such licences (for
reprographic reproduction) may be obtained from the Copyright Licensing
Agency Limited, of 90 Tottenham Court Road, London W1P 9HE.

Typeset by SX Composing DTP, Rayleigh, Essex.
Printed in Great Britain for Hodder & Stoughton Educational, a division of
Hodder Headline Plc, 338 Euston Road, London NW1 3BH by Athenaeum
Press, Gateshead, Tyne & Wear.

1

The Castle

The castle was at the top of a grassy hill.
The sun shone down on the grey stone walls.
It was a hot day
at the end of May.
Guy and Jasmine were tired and hot
by the time they reached the top of the hill.

'What a walk!' said Guy.
'I'm sweating like a pig.'

'It was worth it, though,' said Jasmine.
'Look at the view!'

For miles around you could see
green fields and hills,
lit up in the May sunshine.

'Yeah, great,' said Guy.
He didn't sound as if he meant it.
He hadn't wanted to come.
He thought it was a waste of a Sunday –
travelling all this way to see an old castle.
It was all Jasmine's idea.
She liked history and old things. ,

'Let's go in!' said Jasmine.
The man at the castle gate greeted them.
He wore a tunic and hose,
like they wore in the Middle Ages.
'Seven pounds fifty each,' he said.
'That makes fifteen pounds.'

'Fifteen quid!' grumbled Guy,
reaching for his wallet.
'That's a lot of money –
and I bet it's really boring.'

But Guy was wrong about that.
It wasn't boring.
It wasn't boring at all.

2
The Guide

Through the gate was a small courtyard.
A man stood there.
He was dressed like a soldier
of the Middle Ages.
He wore a leather tunic
and an iron helmet.
A sword hung at his side.

'Good afternoon, my friends,' he said.
'I am your guide.
I will be showing you round
the castle today.'

'Isn't it good, the way they dress up
like it was the olden days?' said Jasmine.

'Yeah, great,' said Guy.
He didn't really mean it.
He thought history was boring.
He'd rather be at home
with a can of beer,
watching a video.
A horror video.
Guy liked horror videos.

More people had joined them now.
There was a little crowd
of about twelve people around the guide.
'The year is 1373,' said the guide.
'I am one of the soldiers of this castle.
As you are guests of the Duke,
it is my duty to show you round.'

Some of the people laughed.
Not Guy, though.
'Follow me!' said the guide.
They followed the guide through an arch.

3

The Dining Hall

_____

'This is the dining hall,' said the guide.
They were in a very big room
with wooden floors and wooden walls.
The walls had carvings on.
A long wooden table ran down
the middle of the room.

'This is where the Duke holds his great feasts,'
said the guide.
'We often have a hundred guests.
They eat roast chicken, roast lamb and
roast wild boar with an apple in its mouth.
Not that I'm invited.
I'm just a soldier.'

Jasmine gazed round the room.
She could just imagine the feast.
She could almost smell it!
Then she gazed up at the ceiling.
'Look at those old timber beams!' she said.
'Yeah, great,' said Guy.

All this talk of roast chicken
was making him hungry.
He wished the tour was over.
Then he could go and get some lunch.

'But it's not all feasting,' said the guide.
'It's not all food and music and dancing.
This is 1373.
These are troubled times.
The Duke has enemies.

And when we capture our enemies,
do you know what we do?'
There was a moment of silence from the group.
'Kill them?' suggested Jasmine.

'In the end, yes,' said the guide.
'But first they have to spend a little time
in the dungeons.
And that's where we're going next.'

Guy perked up a bit at this.
Dungeons.
That was more interesting.
He'd once seen a horror film about a dungeon.
Terrible tortures went on there.
It was really good.

The guide led them out of the dining hall
and down a flight of steep stone steps.
Guy was right behind him.

4

The Dungeon

_____

At the foot of the steps
was a heavy wooden door.
'This is where we keep the prisoners,'
said the guide.

He unlocked the door with a huge iron key.
It opened with a creak.
He led the group down some more steps.
They found themselves in a dark room,
with thick stone walls.
It felt cold and damp.
You couldn't feel the May sunshine
down here.

The guide pointed to some chains
hanging on the walls.
'That's where we chain the prisoners up.
Nobody here at the moment, though.
Just a few rats.'

Jasmine put her arm through Guy's.
'It must have been horrible, mustn't it?'
she said.

'Yeah,' said Guy. 'Horrible!'

'But we don't keep the prisoners chained up
all the time,' said the guide.
'Don't you?' asked Guy.

'No. Sometimes we take them to be tortured.
I'll show you.'

He led the group through another arch
into another stone room.

This room was dark, too,
but there was a red glow
coming from a fire at one end.

Iron instruments, knives and
pincers hung around the walls.
'We heat them up in the fire,
until they're red-hot,' said the guide.

There were iron tables and iron chairs
with chains hanging from them.
'This is where we make
the prisoners comfortable,'
said the guide.
'While we torture them.'
A few people laughed nervously.

'Wow!' said Guy.
'And this really used to go on?'

'Oh, yes,' said the guide.
'Look at this picture.'

5

The Woodcut

A picture hung on the wall.
Quite a small picture –
about thirty centimetres across.
It was an old woodcut,
lit up in the red glow of the fire.

Guy stared at it.
It showed a dungeon –
the same dungeon they were standing in.
Three prisoners were strapped to chairs.
One was strapped to a table.
Another chair was empty.

The picture was crude and simple,
but you could clearly see the pain
on the prisoners' faces.

A torturer stood in the middle.
He had a hood over his face,
and wore thick black gloves.
He was holding red-hot iron pincers.

He looked as if he was wondering
which prisoner to torture next.
The rest of the group gathered round to look.
'Horrible!' said Jasmine.

'Is it real?' asked Guy.
'I mean, is that really what it was like?'

'Oh yes,' said the guide.
'It's fourteenth century.
Probably taken from life.'

'Wow!' said Guy.

'But that's enough torture, I think,'
said the guide.
'Let's go and see the picture gallery.
The Duke has some very fine paintings.'

Guy was the last out of the dungeon.
He kept glancing back at the woodcut.

6

The Picture Gallery

The guide led them to a long gallery,
with pictures hung along the walls.
They were of lords and ladies,
dukes and duchesses.
'This is Lord Burnley,' said the guide.
'And this one is Lady Mary Hilliard.
Here is Sir Stephen Fitzwilliam.
He died in 1408 of eating too many eels.'

'Isn't it interesting?' said Jasmine.

'Yeah, great,' said Guy.
He was getting bored again.

He wanted to go back to the dungeon.
That was the only thing worth looking at.
He knew the guide had not locked the door.
Perhaps he could slip back there.
Have another look at that picture.
He hadn't looked at it long enough before.
Now, he couldn't get it out of his mind.

'Jasmine,' he said quietly.
'I left – er – my jacket in the dungeon.
I'll just slip back and get it.'

'You weren't wearing a jacket!' said Jasmine.
But Guy had already gone.
The guide did not seem to notice.

7

'Who's there?'

Guy pushed the dungeon door open.
He went down the steep stone steps.
He felt strangely excited.
His heart was beating fast.

He went through the room
with the chains on the walls.
Then he went through the stone arch
to the torture room.
The fire cast flickering red shadows
on the walls.
There it was – the woodcut.
Guy went over to look at it.

It's amazing, thought Guy.

So real.

Hard to believe that these people

had suffered and died nearly 700 years ago.

Guy had an idea.

The woodcut was only small.

He could slip it under his shirt.

Then slip out with it.

Steal it, in other words.

Guy wasn't usually a thief.

But there was something about this picture.

He wanted it.

Not to sell.

Just to keep and look at.

He reached out to take the picture

off the wall.

Then he heard a noise.

A footstep.

'Who's there?' said Guy.
He turned round.
A figure was standing there.
He had a black hood over his head.
He wore black leather gloves.

It must be one of the actors, thought Guy.
Dressed up as a torturer.
Guy wondered why he hadn't
shown up earlier.
'Oh, hello,' said Guy.
'I was just . . . having a look round.'
He hoped the man hadn't seen him
about to take the picture.

The torturer didn't say anything.
He stared at Guy for a while.
Then he turned, went through the arch
and locked the dungeon door
from the inside.

8

The Empty Chair

Slowly, the torturer moved towards Guy.
Guy backed away.
'OK, stop trying to scare me.
I know you're only an actor dressed up.
Just open the door for me, please.'

Still the torturer said nothing.
Still he moved towards Guy.
Guy backed away further.
He was up against the wall now.

Guy felt a stab of real fear.

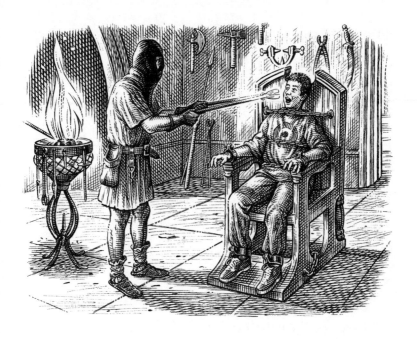

He was on his own down here
with a man dressed up like a torturer.
What if the man was a maniac?

'This isn't funny,' said Guy.
'You'd better let me out.
They'll be waiting for me upstairs.
They'll come looking for me.'

The torturer reached out
and grabbed Guy by the arms.
Guy struggled,
but the man was terrifyingly strong.
He dragged Guy to one of the iron chairs.
He pushed Guy down in it.
He pulled the straps over Guy's arms and legs
and did them up, very tightly.
Guy struggled and kicked,
but it was no use.

'Let me go!' shouted Guy.

Still the torturer didn't say anything.
He went over to the wall
where the torture instruments
were hanging up.
He took down a pair of iron pincers.
He went and held them in the fire.
Soon, they were glowing red hot.

9

A Scream

'This is Sir Harold Hilliard,'
said the guide, pointing at another picture.
'Put to the torture and beheaded in 1392,
for treason.'

Suddenly, a scream rang out.
It was a scream of agony –
a terrible, inhuman scream.
It made Jasmine's blood run cold.

'What's that?' said the guide.
'It seemed to come from the dungeon.'

'Guy's down there!' said Jasmine.
She turned and ran towards the dungeon.
The guide followed.
The screams got louder as they drew near,
then suddenly stopped.

The door was locked.
'I don't remember locking this!'
said the guide.
He got out his key and unlocked it.

He and Jasmine went down
the steep stone steps.
There was no sound now.
They walked through the arch
into the torture room.
Still no sign of anyone.
No sound, except the crackle of the fire.
'Guy? Are you there?' asked Jasmine.

No answer.

There was no sign of Guy anywhere.

Then Jasmine caught sight of the woodcut.
It couldn't be true, but . . .
She took a closer look.
The empty chair was no longer empty.
A man was strapped in it.
The torturer was standing over him with
a pair of red-hot pincers.

The picture was crude and simple,
and the man's face was twisted in pain.
Still, there couldn't be any doubt about it.

Jasmine felt a chill run down her spine
as she stared at the picture.
The man strapped in the chair was Guy.
There couldn't be any doubt about that.